WEEKLY READER CHILDREN'S BOOK CLUB *presents*

# Be Nice to Spiders

*by*

## Margaret Bloy Graham

HARPER & ROW, PUBLISHERS   NEW YORK, EVANSTON, AND LONDON

One morning as the Keeper of the Zoo was about

to unlock the gate, he noticed something on the steps.

It was a matchbox with a note that read:

"Please look after Helen. I've had her since she was a baby,

but I can't keep her anymore. We have to move

to an apartment that won't take pets. Thanks, Billy."

The Keeper opened the matchbox and out jumped Helen.

"Great Scott!" he said. "A spider!"

He tried to catch her, but Helen was too fast for him.

She had eight legs and moved like lightning.

Helen ran up a big maple tree.

Then she quickly spun a long silk thread

and lowered herself into the ventilator

of a big building.

It was the Lion House. There was a big old lion

in one cage and a mother lion and her cubs in another.

There were also lots of flies. They were buzzing

in the lions' ears and crawling on their noses.

The lions were annoyed, but Helen was delighted.
She loved to eat flies. Right away, she set
to work to catch them. She began by spinning a web
with her silk thread.

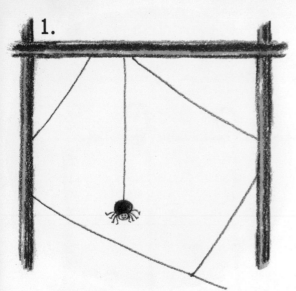

**1.**

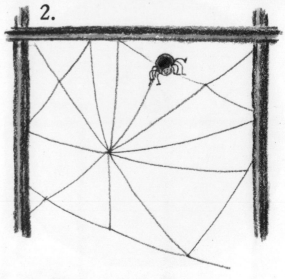

**2.**

First Helen spun the out-
side threads. Then she
dropped straight down.

Next she spun lots of
threads from the center
to the outside.

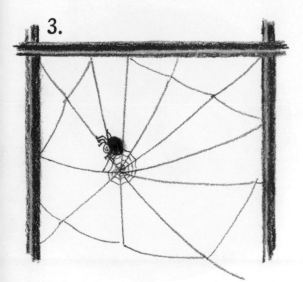

**3.**

**4.**

Then she spun
a little spiral
in the middle.

Finally she spun a big
spiral. This part of
the web was very sticky.

When Helen had finished, she sat in the center
and waited. One by one the flies got caught
in the sticky part of the web.
And one by one Helen ate them.

A week went by. Helen kept catching and eating flies

until there were no more flies in the Lion House.

She had caught and eaten them all!

Now the big old lion snoozed peacefully all day long.

The mother lion licked her cubs and purred.

And Helen was fat and satisfied.

Next Helen moved to the Elephant House.
There were lots of flies there too, and elephants
don't like flies any better than lions do.

In a week Helen had caught all the flies
in the Elephant House. The mother elephant and her baby
were happy and could once again enjoy a bath.

Then Helen moved to the Zebra House.

Flies were crawling all over the zebras

and driving them wild.

As soon as Helen had caught

all the flies there,

the zebras were able to eat their hay in peace.

Helen went from one building to another,

spinning webs and eating up all the flies.

The Zoo became a peaceful place.

All the animals were happy and contented.

As for Helen, she was happy and contented too.

It was a spider's paradise.

One morning the Keeper blew his whistle three times.

All the men came running, and the animals looked up to see

what was going on. "Boys," said the Keeper, "the Mayor

is coming to inspect the Zoo this afternoon at four.

The animals look fine, but the cages sure need cleaning up.

And don't forget to get rid of all those spider webs."

"But, Chief," said his assistant, scratching his head,

"I thought spiders were supposed to be sort of useful."

"Joe," said the Keeper, "those webs make the place

look a mess. OK, boys. Get busy."

The men started sweeping the cages.

Then they hosed and scrubbed them down.

When they were cleaning the Camel House, one of the men
saw Helen. "Quick, give me the broom!" he shouted.

He took a big swing at her, but Helen had disappeared.

The whole Zoo was clean and shining when the Mayor arrived.

"Excellent!" he said. "I'm delighted. I've never seen

the place so neat and the animals looking so well."

Meanwhile Helen was still in the Camel House,

hiding in a crack in the ceiling.

As the days went by she grew very hungry, but she didn't

dare come out. The flies began coming back, and the camels

were irritable again. At last Helen became so hungry

she couldn't stand it any longer. That night, when no one

was around, she started spinning another web.

From then on, Helen stayed in the Camel House,

catching flies. But she didn't dare go anywhere else,

which was lucky for the camels.

They were happy and contented again.

But everywhere else in the Zoo it was a different story.
It didn't take long for the flies to come back and bother
all the other animals. The Keeper went from cage to cage.

"I can't understand it, Joe," he said. "When the Mayor was here, the animals were in such good shape. Now look at them."

"You're right, Chief," said Joe. "They sure look miserable."

Their last stop was the Camel House.

"Why, the camels seem fine," said the Keeper.

"And there don't seem to be any flies in here," said Joe.

They both looked around carefully.

"Look, Chief," Joe shouted. "Now I know what's going on!

See that spider up there? It's eating all the flies.

That's why the camels look so good. Spiders *are* useful.

That's what I tried to tell you the other day."

"Of course, Joe!" cried the Keeper.

"I should have known it all along. Let's call the men."

He blew his whistle, and the men came running.

"Boys," he said, "Joe has made a great discovery.

Spiders are good for the Zoo. They keep the flies

from bothering the animals. They help us do our job.

So from now on there's a new rule: Be nice to spiders."

Soon the Zoo became famous for its happy, healthy animals,

and Helen was treated like a queen.

One day Helen's picture appeared on the front page of the paper.

The headline read: *Local Zoo Named Best of Year;*

*Three Cheers for Spider! Says Keeper.*

That evening the father of the little boy who had left Helen

at the Zoo said, "Billy, look at this."

"Hey, it's my spider!" Billy shouted. "It's Helen!"

"Well, well," said his father, "instead of the Zoo taking

care of Helen, Helen seems to be taking care of the Zoo."

The next morning Billy ran to the Zoo.

"I'm Billy," he said to the Keeper.

"I'm the one who brought you that spider.

Hey, look, she's made an egg sac!

I bet there'll be plenty of baby spiders soon."

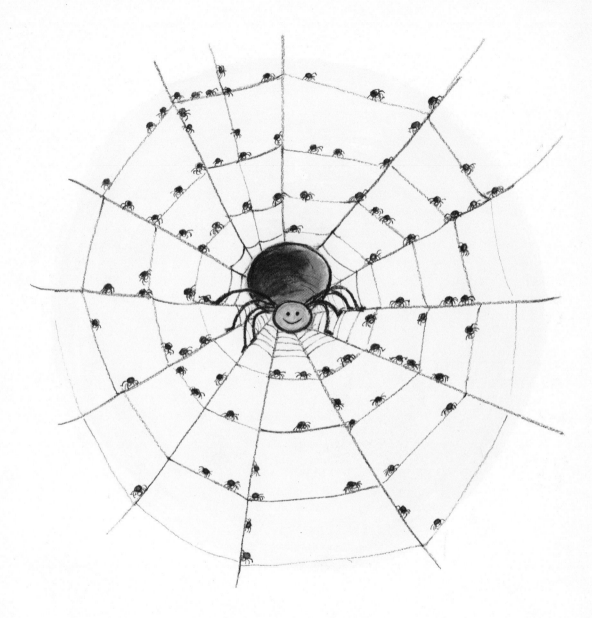

And Billy was right. A few days later,

out of the egg sac came lots of little spiders.

From then on, Helen and her children

and all the animals in the Zoo lived happily ever after.